Dear mouse friends,
Welcome to the world of

Geronimo Stilton

The Editorial Staff of
The Rodent's Gazette

1. Linda Thinslice
2. Sweetie Cheesetriangle
3. Ratella Redfur
4. Soya Mousehao
5. Cheesita de la Pampa
6. Mouseanna Mousetti
7. Yale Youngmouse
8. Toni Tinypaw
9. Tina Spicytail
10. Maximilian Mousemower
11. Valerie Vole
12. Trap Stilton
13. Branwen Musclemouse
14. Zeppola Zap
15. Merenguita Gingermouse
16. Ratsy O'Shea
17. Rodentrick Roundrat
18. Teddy von Muffler
19. Thea Stilton
20. Erronea Misprint
21. Pinky Pick
22. Ya-ya O'Cheddar
23. Mousella Mac Mouser
24. Kreamy O'Cheddar
25. Blasco Tabasco
26. Toffie Sugarsweet
27. Tylerat Truemouse
28. Larry Keys
29. Michael Mouse
30. Geronimo Stilton
31. Benjamin Stilton
32. Briette Finerat
33. Raclette Finerat

Geronimo Stilton
A learned and brainy
mouse; editor of
The Rodent's Gazette

Thea Stilton
Geronimo's sister and
special correspondent at
The Rodent's Gazette

Trap Stilton
An awful joker;
Geronimo's cousin and
owner of the store
Cheap Junk for Less

Benjamin Stilton
A sweet and loving
nine-year-old mouse;
Geronimo's favorite
nephew

Geronimo Stilton

THE CURSE OF THE CHEESE PYRAMID

Scholastic Inc.

New York   Toronto   London   Auckland   Sydney
Mexico City   New Delhi   Hong Kong   Buenos Aires

ISBN 978-0-439-55964-5

Based on an original idea by Elisabetta Dami.

www.geronimostilton.com

Published by Scholastic Inc., 557 Broadway, New York, NY 10012. SCHOLASTIC and associated logos are trademarks and/or registered trademarks of Scholastic Inc.

Stilton is the name of a famous English cheese. It is a registered trademark of the Stilton Cheese Makers' Association. For more information, go to www.stiltoncheese.com.

Text by Geronimo Stilton
Original title *Il mistero della piramide di formaggio*
Illustrations by Matt Wolf
Graphics by Merenguita Gingermouse, Angela Simone, and Benedetta Galante

Special thanks to Kathryn Cristaldi
Interior design by Kay Petronio

36 35 34 33   12 13 14 15 16/0

Printed in the U.S.A.   40
First printing, February 2004

WAKE UP!
WAKE UUUUUUP!

It was just before dawn in the middle of winter. The moon shone down over the mouse holes of New Mouse City. I was fast asleep under my comfy, cozy blankets, snoring away.

Suddenly, the phone rang.

I stumbled out of bed, sinking my paws into my new cat-fur rug. It was so *soft*. I had bought it last weekend at The Fur Mart with my uncle Nibbles. It was expensive, but worth every penny! Still half asleep, I stared down at the fluffy carpet.

Ring!
Ring!
Ring!
Ring!

Then I *picked up* the phone.

"Hello! Stilton speaking, *Geronimo Stilton*," I mumbled.

A strangely familiar voice shrieked back at me. "**WAKE UP!**" it cried.

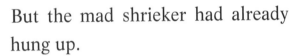

My ears were ringing like church bells at Christmousetime. "W-who . . . w-what . . . who is it?" I stammered.

But the mad shrieker had already hung up.

I glanced at the alarm clock. **RANCID RAT HAIRS!** It was six o'clock in the morning!

I dove back under my covers and continued snoring.

I woke up again at eight o'clock.

I called a taxi to take me to the office.

I arrived at nine o'clock sharp.

Oh, yes, I forgot to mention that I r u n a newspaper. It is called *The Rodent's Gazette.* It is the most popular newspaper on Mouse Island! I'd like to say the paper's a success just because of me. But I have lots of help. Still, I'm the big cheese at the office.

As I was saying, I got to work at nine o'clock sharp. I opened the door to my office wide . . .

. . . and found myself snout-to-snout with my grandfather **William Shortpaws** — also known as **Cheap Mouse Willy**.

Grandfather William is a tough-talking mouse. Everyone at the office is afraid of him. That's because he is the founder of *The Rodent's Gazette*!

My Wallet Bleeds

I barely had taken two pawsteps into the room when Grandfather William began SHOUTING at me. "Graaandson! How dare you arrive at this hour?" he thundered.

I cringed. Where had I heard that shrieking voice before? "But, Grandfather, it's nine o'clock! This is when the office opens," I explained.

Grandfather William just shook his head. "RIDICULOUS!" he cried. "Do you realize you've slept half the day away, Grandson?! I've been here since six o'clock!!!"

A light went on inside my mouse-sized brain. So that was the shrieking voice I had heard on the phone this morning. "Thanks for the wake-up call," I grumbled.

"You're spending too much! Too much! T-o-o m-u-c-h!"

Curling his whiskers, he sniggered with satisfaction. "Now, you listen to me, sonny boy!" he ordered, pulling my ear. "Things are looking bad around here, very bad indeed! Do you know why?"

I opened my mouth to reply, but he didn't give me a chance to answer.

"I'll tell you why!" he bellowed. "Because you're spending too much! **TOO MUCH**! T-o-o m-u-c-h! You must economize! Economize, economize, economize!"

Then he stuck his snout in my ear. "Do you know the meaning of the word, my dear grandson?" he hollered at the top of his lungs. "I'm talking **Economize!**

E as in **END THIS EXTRAVAGANCE IMMEDIATELY!**

C as in **CUT BACK ON ALL EXPENSES!**

O as in **ON YOUR TOES! THINGS ARE ABOUT TO CHANGE!!!**

N as in **NO MORE SPENDING!**

O as in **OH, WHAT A MESS YOU HAVE MADE OF THINGS!**

M as in **MEND YOUR WAYS, GRANDSON, OR I'M TAKING BACK THE FIRM!**

I as in **I FEEL SICK WHEN I HEAR SUCH THINGS!**

Z as in **ZERO, ZILCH, NO SPENDING!**

E as in **ECONOMIZE ON EVERYTHING!**"

Economize!

I gulped. *"Y" as in yikes!* I thought. I guess it wouldn't be a good time to tell Grandfather William about the expensive leather loveseat I had ordered for my office. "B-but, Grandfather . . ." I began.

He pulled my other ear. "Grandfather, my paw! Starting today, I'm keeping track of **EVERYTHING**!" he shouted, waving the account books under my snout. "I expect to see lots of changes. For example, how did you get here this morning?"

I chewed my whiskers. "Well, I took a taxi," I replied.

He slammed his paw on the table. "Exactly! This is what I'm talking about! My wallet **BLEEDS** when I hear such things." He grabbed me by the tie. "Grandson, from now on you'll take the subway to work. No, even better, you can come **ON PAW**. This way, you'll save on the fare and you'll get in first-rat shape!!!"

I felt completely **dazed and confused**. I tried to sit down to catch my breath.

But when I looked around for a chair, I realized Grandfather William had already made some changes. Some perfectly *horrifying* changes! All of my furniture was gone! The desk designed for me by the famous architect Frank Lloyd Rat was nowhere in sight. I whirled around in **shock!** What had happened to my precious leather pawchair, my imported Cheshire cat-fur carpet, my expensive artwork, and my priceless library? The office was empty!

My heart sank like the big ball of cheese in Singing Stone Plaza on New Year's Eve. I had been robbed by my own relative! A plastic table and a plastic chair were the only

pieces of furniture in the whole room!!!

Grandfather looked around, satisfied. "I sold everything to a second-paw dealer," he said with a SMUG SMILE. "You don't need any furniture, just a chair to sit on and a table to write on!"

As he spoke, he banged his paw on the plastic table, which began to WOBBLE.

Quick as a rat half his age, Grandfather caught the table edge before it tipped over. "I may have gray fur," he exclaimed, "but this rodent's not dead yet! I've still got it!"

I swallowed hard. "Grandfather! You sold my precious furniture to a second-paw dealer!" I squeaked. "How much did he give you?"

He waved a wad of money under my snout. "Look at that!" he boasted. "Not bad, huh?"

I counted the money and went PALE!

"But this is way too little! Those were antique books, valuable paintings..." I cried, shaking my head in disbelief. "And they were **MINE!**"

By now my head was spinning. I was in a sad state. I was either going to pull out all of my fur or **sob** like a newborn mouslet.

Grandfather William didn't seem to notice. He stuffed the money back into his wallet.

Then he shouted, "Grandson, you are about to get a lesson in business you'll never forget! Remember, I am the founder of this firm!

FOUNDER OF THE FIRM

I can shut it down with a twitch of my tail!"

I FIRED THEM ALL!

Just then, I noticed something else. The office was so quiet. Where were the reporters, the editors, the proofreaders, and the secretaries? Could they all be taking a coffee break? Somehow, I didn't think so.

I had a terrible feeling.

My whiskers began to tremble. "Grandfather!" I squeaked. "Where is everyone?"

He plopped down on the chair and grinned.

He looked like a cat who had just swallowed a plump Thanksgiving mouse. "I thought you'd never ask, Grandson!" he said, laughing.

He pulled me closer and put his snout up to my ear. "I came up with the most brilliant idea," he whispered. Then he suddenly shouted at the top of his lungs. "I FIRED THEM ALL! Have you any idea how much money we're going to save by getting rid of those CHEESE GUZZLERS?!"

I jumped. Something was ringing, and it wasn't the phone. It was my ear!

"You f-f-f-fired everyone?" I stammered. "But, Grandfather, how are we supposed to run the paper?"

He snorted, waving his paw in the air. "Grandson, I've made up my mind! The paper will be run by the family. Our family. The STILTON FAMILY!" he declared.

Just then, the door banged open and three rodents charged into the office.

The first was my cousin Trap Stilton, also known as Pushy Paws. He is a **plump** mouse with a **LOUD** voice who loves to tell terrible jokes. He's had a ton of different jobs, including ship's cook, cheese taster, stunt mouse, and extra in a horror movie (he played a

My cousin **Trap**

ZOMBIE RAT in the graveyard scene).
Once, he even took a job with the circus,
training fleas to do silly tricks!

Next came my sister, Thea. She is *The
Rodent Gazette*'s special correspondent.
Thea can fly a plane, scuba dive, and ride a
motorcycle. She has a **black belt in karate**.
She has big **violet** eyes and more charm
than last year's Miss Mouse Island! Thea's
got a new **SWEETHEART**
every week. It's true!

That sister of mine
could convince a
starving rat to
give up his last
stick of cheddar
cheese!

My sister, Thea

Of course, Thea is also Grandfather William's **FAVORITE**.

The last mouse in the door was my adorable favorite nephew, Benjamin. He is nine years old and the sweetest, most amazing little mouse ever. Oh, how I love my precious nephew!

Thea's list of victims (I mean boyfriends)

"O, how I love my precious nephew!"

is longer than the tail of a bogeycat.

GERONIMO, DO THIS!
GERONIMO, DO THAT!

Grandfather William eyed us with pride.

"My dear, dear family," he said. "Hold on to your tails. We're about to save more money than Scrooge Rat during the holidays! Let's see . . . first, Geronimo can sort the mail and sweep the floors starting at five in the morning. During the day, Geronimo can also WRITE THE ARTICLES, take them to the printer, answer the phone, make photocopies, go to the post office, et cetera, et cetera, et cetera."

I held up my paw in protest. "Wait a minute. Geronimo, do this! Geronimo, do that! Why do I have to do it all?"

Grandfather William just shook his head sadly. *"Well, cry me a river of cheese,"* he said. "Geronimo, I'm surprised at you! Why can't you be more like your unselfish little sister?" He then began to explain how Thea would be in charge of interviewing all of New Mouse City's VIRs (Very Important Rodents). She would be going to parties and hanging out with celebrity mice while I swept up mouse hairs! I was FUMING. But there was no sense squeaking about it. Thea was Grandfather's darling, and that was that.

To prove my point, my sister twirled around the office, showing off her new designer fur jacket. "Do you like it, Grandfather?" she asked. "I charged it to the paper. After all, I need to look fashionable in my position."

Grandfather William beamed at her with pride. "Of course, my dear, sweet Thea!" he agreed. "You charge anything you want to the paper!"

My sister threw me a smug smile. I bit my tongue. "So much for **economize, economize, economize!**" I muttered under my breath.

Just then, Trap passed Grandfather a basket full of sandwiches. "They're your favorite, Grandfather, blue cheese with extra garlic and red-hot chili peppers!"

Grandfather licked his whiskers and began nibbling away on a sandwich. "This really hits the spot!" he declared. "What would I do without you, my dear grandson?"

Trap winked at me and announced, "Grandfather has hired me to be his personal cook!"

This was ridiculous! I was getting hotter than a bag of cheese popcorn in a microwave. Who would help me run the paper?

At that moment, I felt a tug on the sleeve of my jacket. It was my young nephew Benjamin. "Uncle Geronimo, guess what?" he beamed. "Great-grandfather William has hired me to be his personal assistant!"

Grandfather stroked Ben's tiny ears.

"AH, THE FAMILY, THERE'S NOTHING LIKE THE FAMILY! THE STILTON FAMILY, THAT IS . . ."

I snorted. I could see I was the workmouse of the family. It looked like I would be the *only* one doing any work!

Suddenly, Grandfather whirled around toward me. Uh-oh. What next? Maybe he'd ask me to sharpen all of the *pencils* by paw. Or maybe he'd want me to chop up twigs to make our own paper.

"Geronimo, it seems you are not happy with your duties," he began. *Here it comes,* I groaned silently. "Well, I've got a little *surprise* for you, Grandson," he continued. He stuck a **DC** plane ticket under my snout. "Here you are! I'm sending you on a little trip. That's right. A trip far away from Mouse Island. You're going to Egypt to do a special report on the pyramids!"

I could hardly believe it. I felt like a new mouse! I hate traveling, but I've always wanted to see the pyramids! It was a dream come true!

I stared at the tickets. "Thank you, Grandfather," I said, gasping. "When do I leave?"

He put his snout right up to my ear.

 he screamed.

My ear was ringing again. But this time I didn't care. I was off to *Egypt!*

GOOD LUCK!

I was so excited. It isn't every day a mouse leaves the Island to travel to Egypt!

At the airport, I searched for my ticket counter. "Excuse me, where is the DC Airlines check-in?" I asked a mouse in an airport uniform.

She gave me a look full of pity.

"DC Airlines? You mean Dirt Cheap Airlines?" she said. She pointed to a cardboard box. "Good luck!" she called as I headed for the box.

Good luck??? I repeated to myself. What was that supposed to mean?

Behind the box stood a plump ticket agent with greasy whiskers. She looked me over suspiciously.

"Are you sure you want to get on this flight?"

"Are you sure you want to get on this flight?" **SHE BARKED**. "You're not going to scamper off at the last minute, are you?"

I blinked. "Why would I do that?" I asked, confused.

Just then, a shady-looking mouse approached me. "Hello, my furry friend," he crooned, pumping my paw in a crushing pawshake. "I'm Sammy Slickpaw. But you can just call me Slick."

I winced, checking my paw for broken bones. Slick just grinned wider.

"I'm here to offer you a life insurance policy," he continued. "Did you ever think your plane might CRASH?"

Sammy Slickpaw

I turned **WHITE**. My heart started racing like Mario Mousetti at the track. "Um, well, I try not to think about it," I mumbled.

He nodded gravely. "Well, you really should," he said *softly*. "I mean, one minute these planes are up, the next minute they're down. Do you have any idea how many planes crash each year?"

I gulped. I didn't really want to know.

"Just think," Slick rattled on. "If you had a little life insurance, then your **loved ones** would be taken care of. Come on, sign here and take a load off your mind." He shoved a piece of paper under my snout.

What a slick salesmouse, I thought. But then, I felt a pang in my heart. What would happen to little

What... would happen to little Benj...min?

Benjamin if I were in **Mouse Heaven?** What about his future? Would he end up begging for moldy cheese crumbs instead of heading off to college? Maybe an insurance policy wasn't such a bad idea after all.

I pulled out my pen. But before I could sign the paper, Slick held up a paw. "Just one little question before we do the deal," he said. "You're not flying with **Dirt Cheap Airlines**, are you?"

I blinked. "Um, well, yes. As a matter of fact, I am," I answered.

Quick as a water rat doing the pawstroke, he snatched the paper back.

"Forget it!" he squeaked. "I can't insure anyone flying with them. They're the worst! IT'S FAR TOO RISKY!"

I was beginning to get a terrible twinge in the pit of my stomach. *Oh, what a day!*

CURDLE ME SOUR!!!

Chewing my whiskers, I headed off to find the plane.

A small sign that said Dirt Cheap: DEPARTING FLIGHTS was tacked to the wall. It looked like some mouse had scribbled it with crayons. I turned down a dark hallway. At the end of the hall stood the plane. My fur broke out into a cold sweat when I saw it.

Curdle me sour!!!

Grandfather William had cut costs to the tailbone!

The plane was all PATCHED UP. It looked like it wouldn't make it off the runway!

As I approached, I noticed a mechanic banging his hammer on one of the wings. "There!" he grunted. "Maybe we won't crash this time!"

I gripped my suitcase tightly and climbed on board. A chubby flight attendant took my ticket.

"You're in class Z," she informed me. "Looks like someone's been cutting costs to the tailbone, huh?"

She waved me over to seat number 17. It was a tiny, tattered wicker chair! Instead of a seat belt, there was a piece of STRING! I tried not to scream. Still, my cold sweat had turned into a cold shower!

I sat down carefully. Then I tied my string belt in a double knot. Oh, how did I get myself into this mess? Meanwhile, the plump flight attendant was making an announcement. "Does anyone wish to buy a

"Does anyone wish to buy a parachute?"

Emergency parachute

parachute? This is your last chance! Take 'em or leave 'em!" she snarled.

My whiskers trembled. "A pa-parachute?" I stammered. "But why?"

The flight attendant scowled. "**HELLO IN THERE,**" she called, tapping my head with her paw. "**HAVE YOU SEEN WHAT THIS PLANE LOOKS LIKE?**"

I stared out my broken window. My double-knotted string belt had already snapped in two. Seconds later, I had selected a red-white-and-blue parachute. The flight attendant pointed to the price tag.

"Curdle me sour!!!" I shrieked. The parachute probably cost more than the whole plane!

"Does it matter?" the flight attendant asked. "How much do you value your life?"

With a sigh, I paid. Just as the engines began to buzz, the flight attendant leaned over me. "For the same price, I'll sell you an inner tube, too," she whispered. "I strongly advise it. After all, we'll be flying over the ocean."

Emergency inner tube

One engine started to sputter. It sounded like a cat with a fur ball stuck in its throat. Things were not looking good. I threw more money at the flight attendant and grabbed the inner tube.

Suddenly, a voice screamed over the loudspeaker. "Good morning, rodents! This is your captain, 'Crash' Ratjack! My copilot today is TED SIMPLESNOUT. I'd also like

Captain "Crash" Ratjack

Copilot TED SIMPLESNOUT

"Simplesnout, did you remember to fill up?"

to introduce our flight attendant, **MISS SALLY SKINNYFUR**. In a few minutes, Miss Skinnyfur will be serving you a cheese snack (to everyone except those in class 💤). During the flight, you'll have a chance to watch our movie, *Batmouse and Robin* (except, of course, those in class 💤). The rest rooms are at the rear of the plane (for everyone except those in class 💤, who've been provided with bedpans)."

I peeked under my seat. A metal bowl stared back at me. I crossed my legs and tried not to think of streams, WATERFALLS, or the place where I get my car washed.

As the captain signed off, I tried to relax. But I heard the voices. It was the captain and the copilot speaking. "**SIMPLESNOUT**, did you remember to fill up?" asked the captain.

The copilot let out an ear-piercing squeak.

"Slimy Swiss balls!"

he cried. "I completely forgot, Boss! But we have a tailwind, so we should make it."

"You really think so?" the captain asked with a sigh.

Simplesnout giggled. "Sure. Wanna bet on it, Boss?" he said. "I say with a tailwind, we can just about make it. Anyway, if worse comes to worse we can always do an *EMERGENCY LANDING.* It wouldn't be the first one, right? And besides, over there in Egypt it's full of sand, so we're sure to hit something soft."

The captain groaned. "**SIMPLESNOUT**, you really are short in the brains department," he declared. "But I don't feel like waiting for the fuel truck. Let's just take off and see what happens."

I jumped out of my seat in a panic.

"I WANT TO GET OOOOFFF!"

I squeaked. I headed for the front of the plane.

The flight attendant blocked my way. "CHEESE STICKS! It's too late now, you noodlebrain!" She shoved me back into my seat. "We're about to take off!"

The engines buzzed more loudly. The plane took off down the runway. Then it wobbled into the air.

I let out a silent scream.

My fur stood on end.

IT REALLY WAS TOO LATE.

Too late to get off the plane. Too late to switch flights. Too late to show Grandfather William who the *real* boss was. I was risking my life on a plane with no fuel, flown by two wacky pilots.

Oh, what a day!!!

HOW DO YOU DO?
I'M DANIEL E.
DEADFUR!

The plane took off with a sputter and a cough. For the next two hours, we sailed along without a problem.

Then, all of a sudden, the plane began shaking. No, I don't mean a polite little trembly kind of **shaking**. I'm talking about violent, jerky shaking. It reminded me of the time I got locked in my great uncle Coldpaw's walk-in freezer overnight. I was shaking so hard from the cold I was seeing double! By the time they found me, I looked like a furry Fudge Pop!

Miss Skinnyfur's voice interrupted my

thoughts. "Passengers are kindly requested to hold their passports between their teeth," she instructed. "This way, your fur will be easily identified in case we cra5h."

I gripped my wicker chair tightly. Maybe if I tried humming a tune I would feel better, I decided. Yes, a *happy little jingle* might do the trick. But before I could think of one, the mouse behind me beat me to it. Only he wasn't humming a **happy** tune. He was humming a song that made grown mice cry. It was called "Good-bye, Sweet Cheese, Good-bye."

I turned around. I was snout-to-snout with a very odd-looking mouse. He wore a black wig and was dressed

Daniel E. Deadfur

all in purple from his tail to his whiskers. His mustache drooped **sadly** over his snout. He wore a very unusual watch on his paw. It had a picture of an open coffin with a smiling mouse lying inside! He was reading a book with a dusty cover. It was called *A Rodent's Guide to the World's Most Beautiful Cemeteries.* I gulped. I wouldn't want to run into this mouse in a dark alley. He was creepier than a **GHOST** cat on Halloween!

"Allow me to introduce myself," the sad mouse said in a gloomy tone. "My name is Daniel E. Deadfur. I'm an undertaker."

"Passengers are kindly requested to hold their passports between their teeth."

I nodded. Now I knew why old Deadfur was so depressed. He spent his days staring at stiffs!

With a heavy sigh, the unhappy mouse stared out the window. "Looks like we might **crash**," he predicted. "Oh, well, I guess you win some, you lose some."

My whiskers stood on end. *"HOLEY CHEESE!"* I croaked.

The undertaker blinked. "You sound surprised," he said, startled. "You must know air travel is very, very, very dangerous. Plus, we're sitting right on top of the wing. Did you know the wing is the most **DANGEROUS** place to be when *a plane goes down?"*

By now, I felt faint. I tried taking deep breaths, but my lungs didn't seem to be working. Spots swam before my eyes.

"No!" I screamed.

*"I'M TOO YOUNG TO GO!
I HAVEN'T CLIMBED
MOUSE EVEREST YET!*

I haven't trekked through the Great Mousewood Forest! And besides, I still have a whole unopened package of cheddar cheese bars at home in my fridge!"

Too bad no one heard me. I was so scared, I had completely lost my squeak!

FROZEN WITH FEAR!

Terrified, I squeezed my special lucky charm. It was a **silver** four-leaf clover. My nephew Benjamin had given it to me for my birthday. A tear slid down my fur. I wondered if I would ever see my beloved nephew again.

The plane was jumping up and down like my sister, Thea, in her step class at Rats La Lanne. I was **frozen with fear**! Why, oh, why did I get on this rattrap of a plane?!

Just as I was about to drown in my own tears, we stopped bouncing. The flight attendant made an announcement. "The turbulence is over!" she squeaked. "Passengers are requested to

Terrified, I squeezed my special lucky charm.

keep their seat belts fastened. We'll be landing in half an hour."

I heaved a sigh of relief. *I knew we would make it,* I told myself. But, of course, I spoke too soon. Seconds later, disaster struck. The engines DIED. The silence was sickening.

"What did I tell you, Simplesnout?" the captain's voice squeaked. "I won the bet. I told you the fuel wouldn't last."

I could hear the copilot grumbling. "OK, Boss. I guess you won. Looks like we need to try that emergency landing again." He sighed.

My eyes popped open.

EMERGENCY?? LANDING??

"Heeelp!" I shrieked. I couldn't take it anymore. My nerves were shot.

What did I do to deserve this ending? I tried to be a good big brother to Thea. I know I was a doting uncle to Benjamin. And then, of course, there was my cousin Trap. Well, I guess I could try to be a better cousin. But Trap was so annoying. He loved to play mean jokes on me. Like on my birthday, when he put hot **CHILI** peppers in my cheesecake.

I stared out my broken window. *Think positive,* I told myself.

The plane circled over the ocean, then it headed for the desert. It looked like we were about to dive straight into the **sand!** I squeezed my eyes shut. Then, suddenly, I heard a **NOISE.** Could it be? It was! The engines had started up again!

With a jolt, we finally reached Cairo airport. Wobbling, I headed for the exit.

"**Crunchy cheese chunks!** What a nightmare!" I squeaked. "I'm surprised I didn't die of fright!"

Daniel E. Deadfur scampered after me. "If you think you're about to go, just give me a call," he said. He handed me his card.

I shook my head and bolted out the door.

Oh, what a day!

PROFESSOR ALRAT SPITFUR

In the airport, I read Grandfather William's instructions again. I had to interview Professor **ALRAT SPITFUR**. He had invented a new way to create energy. I wondered what it could be. I loved hearing about scientific discoveries. Then I could write about them in my paper.

I was getting into a taxi when my cell phone rang. "Hello! This is Stilton, *Geronimo Stilton*," I answered.

Grandfather's voice blew out my eardrum. "ROTTEN RATS' TEETH!" he shrieked. "Did you not hear one word I said, Grandson?! Am I talking just to hear my own voice?

Doesn't anyone listen anymore?

If a tree fell in a forest and no one was around, would it make a sound?"

I stared at the phone. I had no idea what my grandfather was babbling about. "You're on a **budget!**" he squeaked at last. "Forget the taxi, Grandson! Hire a camel! And don't forget to ask for a discount!"

I haggled with a camel driver. Then I climbed in between the camel's humps.

One thing you should know about riding a camel, it's just like being on a boat.

GLBBB...

I was soon seasick.

Yes, I, *Geronimo Stilton*, got seasick on dry land!

Oh, what a day!

I reached the laboratory an hour later. By that time, I looked like a tired lump of moldy green cheese.

The lab was a **CONCRETE** building sitting in the middle of the desert. I lurched up the steps and rang the doorbell. And that's when it hit me. The most horrible **SMELL** you could ever imagine. I held my breath. It was unbearable.

By the time the door opened, I was turning blue. A funny-looking rodent with red fur and thick glasses peered out at me. He wore a white lab coat and had a clothespin on his nose.

PROFESSOR ALRAT SPITFUR

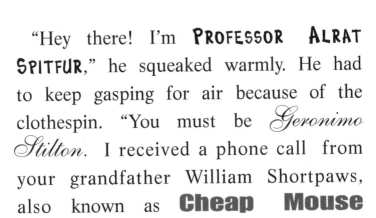
"Hey there! I'm **PROFESSOR ALRAT SPITFUR**," he squeaked warmly. He had to keep gasping for air because of the clothespin. "You must be *Geronimo Stilton*. I received a phone call from your grandfather William Shortpaws, also known as **Cheap Mouse Willy**. He must be some mouse!"

"Yes, I am *Geronimo Stilton*. And you're right, my grandfather is some mouse," I gasped. "Some kind of crazy, wacko, infuriating mouse," I added under my breath.

The professor pulled a clothespin out of his pocket. "You might want to wear this," he advised. "Now, come along. I'll show you around the LABORATORY."

I realized the STENCH was getting stronger and stronger. I quickly stuck the clothespin on my nose.

Professor Spitfur led me into a stable. It was where they bred hundreds of camels. You wouldn't believe the stink!

Professor Spitfur began to explain about his incredible discovery. "You

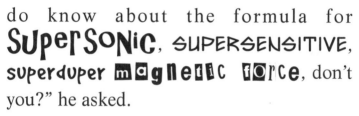

do know about the formula for **SuperSONic**, SUPERSENSITIVE, superduper **magnetic force**, don't you?" he asked.

As he spoke, I had to keep hopping back and forth. It turns out the professor wore dentures. Every time he opened his mouth, streams of ratspit shot out at me! I know I needed a shower after my flight, but this was ridiculous! *Oh, what a day!*

OH, WHAT A DAY!

Inside the stable, the camels looked harmless enough. They stood peacefully together making strange GURGLING sounds.

I pulled out my notebook and began taking notes: *Meek, mild creatures. Sound like they are blowing bubbles underwater.* I approached one to get a closer look.

"Be careful!" the professor quickly warned me. "Never look a camel straight in the eye! They love to **spit**. And they're wonderful **shots**!"

The camel whipped his snout around toward me and SPIT!

I immediately jumped back. But it was too late.

The camel whipped his snout around toward me and SPIT! He hit me right in the eye.

"Yuck!" I groaned, wiping my eye with my paw. It was bad enough I had to dodge the professor's spit. Now I had to worry about the camels' spit, too!

"See? I told you!" splattered the professor, shaking his head.

I decided to stay away from the camel's snout. I snuck behind the second camel. This one didn't spit on me. Instead, he kicked me right in the tail!

Crying out in pain, I took a step backward. Right into a pile of camel dung!!!

I slipped on the dung, did a **triple** somersault, and bruised my snout when I hit the ground!

Oh, what a day! What a day! What a day! What a day!

Ouch!

I snuck behind the camel.
He kicked me
right in the tail.

Double
ouch!

I took a step backward,
right into a pile of
camel dung!!!

Ouchie!
Ouchie!
Ouchie!

I slipped on the dung,
did a triple somersault .

Oouuucccchhh!!!

and bruised my snout
when I hit the ground.

WHAT A SMELL, WHAT A STENCH, WHAT A STINK!

Just then, Professor **SPITFUR** began shrieking.

"Look out! What are you doing? That's very precious raw material!" he cried.

I scanned the stable, scratching my fur.

"W-what? What **raw material?**" I stammered. The **SMELL** in the stable was making me dizzy. I felt faint. It was worse than the time my grouchy Grandma Onewhisker burned her revolting blue cheese and gouda casserole.

The professor lowered his voice as if he were about to let me in on a **BIG SECRET**.

"You must have figured it out by now, right?" he whispered. "The raw material I use to produce energy is camel dung!"

He dragged me out of the laboratory. Then he pointed to a yellow building in the shape of a Swiss cheese pyramid. Smelly brown smoke drifted out from its chimney. Beside the pyramid stood some huge solar panels.

"I use the sun to fuel the boiler. Then I ferment the camel dung," the professor explained. "The fumes turn on an engine that creates energy!"

I gasped, choked by the fumes. What a SMELL, what a stench, what a stink!

I'm never going to get this stink out of my fur, I thought. *No one will want to sit next to me on the plane ride home. They'll have to hand out clothespins to the other passengers. Or maybe they'll give me a special seat — attached to the outside of the plane!* Oh, well. I couldn't worry about that now. I was getting too excited about the professor's discovery. It looked like his invention really worked! I glanced down at my notes. "Professor **SPITFUR**, are you saying that camel dung can make **ENERGY?**" I asked.

The professor shook his head and chuckled. "Well, not exactly," he explained. "You see, you also need a secret ingredient. A strictly HUSH-HUSH INGREDIENT that I hide in here!"

As he spoke, he hit his forehead with his paw.

I kept on writing: *"ingredient . . . big secret . . . in here . . ."*

"Yes, Stilton," the professor splattered on. "I keep the secret inside my creaky old brain, my noggin, my think box! And do you know, Stilton, where I got the idea for this secret ingredient from? Do you, Stilton?! Well, *do you?!*"

"I use the sun to fuel the boiler.

I hopped about. The professor was getting more excited than a cat on a Royal Rodent luxury cruise ship. He was spitting up a *storm!*

"No," I answered, trying to avoid another shower of rat saliva. "How should I know?"

The professor lowered his voice again and squeaked, "I got the idea from the ancient writing inside CHEOPS's pyramid!"

Then I ferment the camel dung."

THE EYE OF RA

My ears perked up. CHEOPS was one of the great pharaohs of Egypt. The pyramid that Cheops was buried inside was the biggest one ever built!

Now I was getting really excited. Mostly because I was going to learn more about an amazing pyramid. But also because a **breeze** had started blowing. The professor and I were able to take off our clothespins. I rubbed my nose, then continued scribbling in my notebook.

"I'm really an *Egyptologist*," the professor explained. "That means I'm an expert in *Egyptian* culture. Anyway, one day I was inside the Cheops pyramid, studying some hieroglyphs, when I got my idea. The ancient writings showed pictures of lots of camels and a sun. It was the eye of Ra. I started thinking about camels and the sun. An idea started buzzing in my head. Maybe the two could work together to make *ENERGY!*"

The professor showed me an old piece of paper covered with painted symbols. There were flowers, boats, crocodiles, owls, even cats. "These are hieroglyphs," he said. Then he scratched his fur. "Say, I have an idea. Would you like to visit CHEOPS's pyramid, Stilton?" he asked.

My eyes opened wide. Would a mouse like cheesecake on his birthday? "I sure would!" I squeaked.

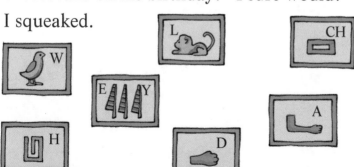

THE SECRET OF THE PYRAMIDS

We mounted two camels standing outside the lab and galloped off. The sun was setting over the desert sand, painting the dunes pink.

I pulled out my camera. Somehow I managed to take a few great shots without falling off the camel.

click   click
    click

Oh, what a day!

After a wild ride, we finally spotted Cheops's

pyramid.

The professor jumped off his camel and parked it like a pro.

I slid off mine and crumpled to the ground. My snout was GREEN from the crazy ride.

CHEOPS

CHEPHREN

MYKERINOS

"*HOLEY CHEESE! . . .*" I murmured. My camel gave me a look that said, *You are one sorry, sorry mouse, Stilton.*

I wasn't sure why we had stopped, but I quickly found out. It seemed the professor had a little history lesson in store for me. He began to recite. "The pyramids were

FUNERARY monuments dedicated to the pharaohs, like Cheops, Chephren, and Mykerinos. The pyramids have a **SQUARE** base. Inside, there are one or more burial chambers connected by secret corridors and passages.

SQUARE SQUARE SQUARE SQUARE SQUARE

"After his death, the pharaoh's body would be emptied of its internal organs. It was then treated with a special substance called *mum* to preserve it. Finally, it was wrapped in linen bandages and placed in a sarcophagus, a big stone coffin.

"The pharaoh's mummy was sealed inside the sarcophagus. Then, all of the pharaoh's riches were placed around it. That's because the Egyptians believed that after death, the soul went on a journey to the afterlife, taking all its *treasures* with it! Robbers have been digging through the pyramids for centuries, looking for the riches left beside the pharaohs' sarcophagi.

"The pyramids are still a great MYSTERY to this day. They were built thanks to the labor of thousands of workers. Most of them were peasants. The peasants built these huge monuments to honor their pharaoh.

"Cheops's pyramid is the biggest stone structure ever built. How were the Egyptian workers able to lift such incredibly heavy blocks? No one knows for sure. Perhaps the workers transported the blocks using wooden rollers to slide them along!"

Professor Spitfur coughed. Then he added in a low voice, "According to some theories, the Egyptians lifted the blocks by the use of telepathy, or the power of thought. It is said

*"Perhaps the workers transported
the blocks using wooden rollers."*

they built the pyramids to honor aliens from some faraway galaxy."

I glanced up at the **sky**. I hoped the aliens didn't decide to pay us a visit. I had enough trouble trying to handle my came*l*. Forget extra-terrestrials!

Oh, what a day!

The Pyramids are still a great mystery to this day.

The Pharaoh's Curse

The professor pointed toward a tunnel on one side of the pyramid.

"We're going this way," he said. "Don't forget your camera! This place is a sight to make you **squeak!**"

I gripped my camera and followed in the professor's pawsteps. The ceiling was so low my ears brushed the ceiling! I shuddered. I hate being in small, tight spaces. Oh, well, there was no time to think about it now. The professor was spewing out information like a walking encyclopedia salesmouse.

"Legend has it," he began in a mysterious tone, "that whoever desecrates a pharaoh's tomb falls victim to a terrible curse! For example, in 1922, two Englishmice discovered Tutankhamen's tomb in the Valley of the Kings. Inside, they found priceless treasures: the pharaoh's magnificent mask, his mummy, a solid-gold sarcophagus, and also many statues, jewels, and precious stones. Twenty-six mice witnessed the discovery. Many of them died in a mysterious way in the following years. That is how the legend of the curse was born!"

A shiver ran through my fur. All this talk about curses and death was giving me the creeps. I started taking *pictures* click click click even though my paws were shaking.

Meanwhile, the professor let out a low **chuckle**. "By the way, Stilton, did you know I, too, discovered a tomb a month ago?" he said. "But nothing has happened to me. I'm still kicking up the old paws. I don't give a whisker about all these legends. It's just total **nonsense**."

At that precise moment, something horrible happened! The professor tripped on a stone and smashed his snout on the ground. His flashlight went out.

The room was totally dark.

A dreadful silence followed.

"Professor! Professor!" I cried. But there was no answer.

I took a couple of pawsteps forward. Big mistake. I tripped and hit the ground with a thud. I looked around. It was dark. Pitch-black dark. I couldn't even see my own whiskers next to my nose. How would I be able to find the exit?

HOLEY CHEESE! I was hopelessly lost!

BASTET, THE CAT GODDESS

I crawled along the floor. I wanted to get back to the tunnel entrance, but I wasn't sure which way to go. My fur stood on end. My paws shook. Even my tail twitched with fear.

"Professor! Professor Spitfur!" I squeaked again, this time in a total panic.

But there was only silence.
A SPOOKY, TOMBLIKE SILENCE!

Now I was shaking. I felt like a mouse who gets kicked out of his hole in the middle of winter. I needed a pep talk. Unfortunately, I seemed to be the only one around to give it. *You're going to be fine! There's absolutely nothing to worry about!*
I told myself.

It didn't work. Seconds later, I was bawling my eyes out.

WHAT AM I GOING TO DO?!
I cried.

My words echoed in the dark. Finally, I remembered the key ring in my pocket. On it was a small flashlight.

I switched it on.

The light gave me courage. It lit up the wall in front of me.

I jumped. A jackal-headed monster moved toward me, ready to pounce!

"Slimy Swiss balls!!" I shrieked in terror.

But then, I bent to get a better look. It wasn't a real monster. It was a painting.

I recognized a drawing of the jackal-headed ANUBIS. On his right stood OSIRIS,

The small flashlight lit up the wall in front of me.

god of the underworld, and his wife, Isis. There was also a drawing of their son, Horus, god of the sky and of light, whose head is that of a falcon. But what was that animal at the bottom? I stepped closer to the wall to get a better look. **Yikes!** I was looking directly into the face of Bastet, the cat-headed goddess.

Moldy mozzarella!

CATS SCARE ME OUT OF MY WITS!!!

ANUBIS HATHOR RA ATUN ISIS OSIRIS HORUS

I wanted to race out of that pyraMid as fast as my paws would take me, but I had to be brave and find the professor. If I didn't, he'd wind up a mummy mouse!

I looked at the painting again. There were many more pictures—of pharaohs and priests, soldiers and scribes, farmers and artisans. And they were all more than five thousand years old! It was truly *amazing*. Of course, I would've enjoyed the artwork much more if my tail hadn't been trembling with terror. **HOW WOULD I EVER GET OUT OF THIS TOMB?**

PHAROAH

PRIESTS

SOLDIERS

SCRIBES

ARTISANS AND FARMERS

INVENTION?
WHAT INVENTION?

Suddenly, I saw the professor lying on the ground. He wasn't moving.

"Professor! Are you all right?" I cried.

The professor still didn't move. But something else was moving right next to him. It slithered along the floor, hissing. I **shivered**.

It was a snake!

Could this be the pharaoh's curse? Was Spitfur being punished because he had discovered that tomb last month?

Of course not, I told myself. Those were just silly old legends.

I took a deep breath and grabbed the professor. In a flash, the snake flicked out ITS FORKED TONGUE.

Poisonous cheese puffs! It was getting ready to strike!

Just then, I remembered something I had read in a book about snakes. I quickly stamped my paw on the ground. It worked! The snake was frightened by the vibrations, and it took off. My cousin Trap always makes fun of me for being a *brainy mouse*. But, as you can see, it pays to be well read!

With a groan, I dragged the professor all the way back to the entrance of the tunnel. I felt like I was pulling a ten-pound block of cheddar. **He was one heavy rat!**

At last, my snout peeped out of the pyramid. A few minutes later, Professor Spitfur opened his eyes.

"Professor, how do you feel?" I cried.

The professor rubbed his snout. "I'm fine, just fine," he mumbled. "But who are you?"

I blinked. "D-d-d-don't you r-r-r-recognize me, Professor? I'm Stilton, *Geronimo Stilton*," I stammered.

He shook his head, scratching his red whiskers.

"I'VE NEVER SEEN YOUR SNOUT BEFORE."

"You don't remember taking me to see Cheops's pyramid?" I asked. "You were going to explain to me how your extraordinary invention was born."

He gaped. "**WHAT?** Invention?" he repeated. "What invention???"

"The invention of the thingy, I mean, of the camel dung!" I squeaked.

Professor Spitfur just stared at me. "Dung? Camel?" he murmured. "My dear young mouse, are you sure you're feeling all right? You didn't by any chance bash your head, did you?" He waved his paw in front of my eyes. "How many paws do you see?" he asked me.

What ingredient?

"Professor!" I shrieked. "You're the one who bumped his head!"

"Maybe. But I don't remember a thing. . . ." He sighed.

I pulled at my fur. "Of all the rotten rat luck! Does this mean you don't remember the secret ingredient? The one that you added to the camel dung to make energy?!"

I stared into his eyes. He stared back. For a minute, he seemed like he might remember me. Then he opened his mouth to squeak. "What ingredient? What dung? What camel? *WHAT ENERGY?*"

A FLOATING PIECE OF DYNAMITE

It had been a terrible day. I had come to Egypt to get a scoop, but I was going home empty-pawed!

I looked at my watch. HOLEY CHEESE! It was already five o'clock in the morning. The sun was rising on the horizon.

What an amazing sight!

Now I understood why the Egyptians worshiped the sun. They gave it several names: Ra, Atum, Amon. They even built obelisks to honor the sun. I took several pictures. Then I packed my things. It was time to head back home to New Mouse City.

Obelisk

I said good-bye to the professor, who unfortunately could not remember anything about his invention. Oh, well. *It wasn't every day a mouse got to see a real Egyptian pyramid,* I told myself. I climbed onto my camel and galloped to the airport.

Just as I was pulling up to the plane, my cell phone rang. It was Grandfather William. "**Grandson!**" he squeaked. "You're not thinking of flying back, are you? *You're* BLEEDING *me dry!* Have you forgotten my little lesson in saving money already? You'll come back by boat!"

I groaned. I wasn't really in the mood for a long boat ride, but Grandfather had his mind made up. "Go to the harbor!" he barked. "I've already booked your return ticket."

I galloped all the way to the harbor, where I discovered that Grandfather

It was a horrible journey.

had bought me a ticket on a cargo ship. It was called the *Dynamiter.*

I climbed on board.

For some reason I had a funny feeling about that ship. I soon found out why. It was packed with deadly **EXPLOSIVES!** One wrong move and we'd be fried mice!

It was a horrible journey. No luxury cruise for this mouse, that's for sure. I was stuck on a rickety old ship with sticks of dynamite as bunkmates. Yes, once again Grandfather William had cut costs to the tailbone!

The captain of the ship was a rodent named Squeaky Kaboom, but everyone

Squeaky Kaboom

called him Boom for short. He was a gray-furred mouse with a long scar on his snout and drooping whiskers. Boom loved to tell awful jokes. His great booming laugh could be heard day and night. Whenever he saw me, he would slap me on the shoulder and squeak: "Be careful with **MATCHES**, Stilton! We're a floating piece of dynamite here! Hey, why are you so *PALE?* Ha-ha, ha-ha!"

I could hardly believe I was stuck on this rattrap of a ship for one whole month! Why,

oh, why had I wanted to go to Egypt?! It was bad enough that I never got the story from Professor Spitfur, **but now, to top it off, I was seasick.** You see, I'm really not a sea mouse. I'm a land mouse at heart. I spent most of the journey home curled up in my bunk, shivering. Even my whiskers felt nauseous!

I could not wait to get back home to New Mouse City.

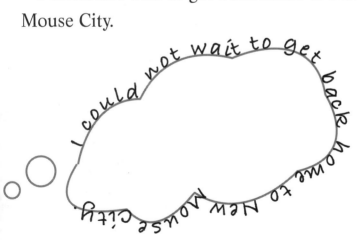

PSSST, PSSSSSSST . . . HEY, STILTON!

At last, we reached New Mouse City's harbor. I jumped off the boat and raced straight to *The Rodent's Gazette.* I couldn't wait to see how things were going at the office!

I was on my way up the stairs when I heard someone whisper, "Psssst, Stilton! Over here!"

I turned the corner and bumped right into Shif T. Paws. Shif is the sales manager of *The Rodent's Gazette.* I

don't know how the paper would run without him.

THAT MOUSE WAS
ONE OF A KIND.

He could sell papers to a rabid tomcat!

"Shif!" I squeaked. "It's so great to see you. I'm sorry Grandfather William fired you."

Shif just smirked and stroked his whiskers. His beady eyes shone behind metal-rimmed glasses.

"Don't worry, Mr. Stilton!" he cried. "As it turns out, I was the **only one** to be rehired!"

Shif T. had agreed to work for free.

BLUE CHEESE SHAKES AND TRIPLE CHEDDAR BURGERS

I was shocked. Grandfather William never changed his mind. It was stuck on one track like the train at Little Whiskers Fun Park. Was he turning over a NEW LEAF? Was he finally changing his cheaprat ways? Was I about to sprout wings and fly all over Mouse Island? I shook my head. Not a chance. Shif T. must have some slick trick up his paw, I decided.

I was right. It seemed that the salesmouse had agreed to work for free.

Of course, Grandfather William agreed. After all, *free* was one of his favorite words!

"But don't worry, Mr. Stilton," Shif added. "I have a *fabumouse* plan!"

I took Shif up on his offer to talk about the plan over lunch. We headed off to The Ratburger. We ordered two blue cheese shakes and two **TRIPLE** cheddar burgers. Then Shif leaned in close and explained his plan to get back *The Rodent's Gazette.*

It was a good one.

We left The Ratburger two hours later.

Shif T. slapped me a high-five. "Ready, Mr. Stilton?" he asked.

"**READY, SHIF***!*" I squeaked with a grin. Yes, we were ready, all right. We had cheese in our bellies and a plan to send Grandfather packing.

WE WERE READY FOR ANYTHING

FRIENDS TOGETHER!
MICE FOREVER!

We scampered back to *The Rodent's Gazette.* Then we snuck in through the back door. We were quiet as mice. The office was quiet, too. No one was tapping on the ⌨ c o m p u t e r . No one was squeaking on the phone. No one was using the fax machine. It was spooky. *The Rodent's Gazette* was **slowly closing down.**

"This place is emptier than my auntie Slimrat's refrigerator," whispered Shif T.

We crept into the editorial room. A mouse sat in the corner. It was my sister, Thea!

"Pssst! Thea!" I whispered.

"Geronimo!" she squeaked. "I'm so happy to see you!"

I motioned for her to keep quiet. I didn't want Grandfather William to hear us.

Thea slipped under the desk. Shif T. and I followed.

"I can't stand it any longer!" Thea complained. "Grandfather's ideas are so old-fashioned. He's completely behind the times. We have to **DO SOMETHING**!"

"Shif T. Paws has a plan," I explained.

Suddenly, another rodent's snout peeped under the desk. "What's shaking, Cousinkins?" a voice called. It was my cousin Trap. He thumped me on the back. Hard.

I tried to remember what I had told myself on the plane. Be nice to your cousin. He's a relative, after all.

I took a deep breath. "We've got a plan to get rid of Grandfather William," I told Trap.

My cousin rolled his eyes. "*HOLEY CHEESE!*

He's worse than the warden at **Ratcatraz Prison**," he groaned. "He won't even let us take Saturday or Sunday off! Count me in!"

Just then, another snout peeped under the desk.

"Uncle Geronimo! You're back!" my nephew cried. He threw his paws around my neck. "**I missed you so much, Uncle,**" Benjamin squeaked. "I mean, I didn't mind being Great-grandfather's assistant, but he can be a little bit pushy. I'm so glad you're back!"

I grinned. It looked like Operation Rodent Freedom was on!

To seal the deal, we twisted our tails together and squeaked, "Friends together! Mice forever!"

I'm Such a Genius!

Like James Bondrat on a secret mission, we snuck into my office. Grandfather sat behind the small plastic table.

He was muttering in an angry tone. **"THUNDERING CATTAILS**! Just look at these expenses! Who would think toilet paper could cost so much?! My wallet **BLEEDS** to see such things!"

He scratched his furry head. Then his eyes lit up. "I've got an **Idea**," he shouted. "Starting today, we'll give up toilet paper. We'll use old newspaper sheets instead. That will cut down on our costs. Perfect! I'm such a genius!"

He was very pleased with himself. He really was one

special mouse — especially cheap, that is!

Grandfather stared back at the books, frowning.

"We still need to s-a-v-e m-o-n-e-y!" he mumbled. "Let's see, I could work out a time mechanism for the toilets. When a mouse goes to the bathroom, the door will open after thirty seconds. Either you're done or you're wasting precious time! Ha-ha-haaa! I could also hide the coffee machine so no one will waste time taking a coffee break. Hmmm. I could even turn off all the electricity.

"Wait a minute," he continued, twisting his whiskers in a knot. "If I **cut** the electricity, then the computers wouldn't

work." He frowned again. But after a few seconds, he slammed the table with his paw. "Who cares!" he declared. "We'll just go back to using *typewriters. Just like the old days!* Ha-ha-haaa!"

At that moment, Thea jabbed me with her elbow. "I told you," she hissed. "Grandfather's gone off the **DEEP END**. He's lost his marbles. The **CHEESE** has slipped off his cracker. We've got to stop him!"

I nodded. We had to do something right away. We all loved Grandfather. Still, his crazy cost-cutting ideas were about to ruin his own newspaper!

Just then, Shif T. Paws spoke up. "Let's go to the phone," he declared. "It's time to put our plan into action!"

WHO'S PAYING???

We crowded around the phone. This was it. I nodded to Thea. She put a clothespin on her nose and dialed Grandfather's number.

"Hellooo! Is this Mr. Shortpaws?" my sister said in a funny voice. I held my breath. Hopefully, Grandfather would not realize the caller was his favorite grandchild.

"**yes!** I'm Shortpaws, **William Shortpaws!**" Grandfather thundered. Thea held up the phone so we could hear his response.

"Mr. Shortpaws," Thea continued. "I'm calling from the **ROYAL WATER RATS CRUISE LINE**. I've got some great news for you. Do you have a minute?"

Grandfather snorted. "A minute?" he

scoffed. "I don't even have a second! Time is money and money is time! I'm trying to **RUN A BUSINESS** here! Tell me what you want or I'm hanging up!"

With a squeak, Trap snatched the phone away from Thea. Thea snatched it back. They began to wrestle silently over the phone. I put my head in my paws. Those two loved to fight as much as I loved my precious petrified cheese collection!

At last, Shif T. Paws grabbed the phone. "MR. SHORTPAWS, MY MOUSE," he boomed in a deep voice. "I'm the owner of the **ROYAL WATER RATS CRUISE LINE**. How are you

today?" He didn't give Grandfather a chance to reply. "I have wonderful news for you. You are the first-prize winner of a *fabumouse* world tour on one of our cruise ships!"

Grandfather gasped. "But who's paying?"

"We are, of course. **ROYAL WATER RATS CRUISE LINE**. Everything is free, Mr. Shortpaws," Shif rambled. "Your ticket will be waiting for you at the harbor. But you must leave right away. Otherwise, we'll have to give your prize to another lucky mouse!"

Suddenly, we heard an ear-piercing shriek. "Noooooo! Don't give it to anyone else, it's mine!" Grandfather screamed. "Mine, mine, mine! I've never won anything in my life. *HOLEY CHEESE!* **A free trip around the world?** How could I refuse? I knew someday my ship would come in!" Grandfather chuckled at his own bad joke. He slammed down the phone. Then he rushed out the door.

I stuck my head into my office. Grandfather had left us a note:

The party is over!
No more counting on Grandfather.
You're on your own now.
But watch your step.
I've got my eye on you!

I sighed. Grandfather really did need a break. A little vacation would do him good. And a free **vacation** was his favorite kind! He would never know we had all chipped in to send him away. Of course, even a cruise around the world wouldn't keep Grandfather away forever. But at least we'd have our toilet paper for a little while.

CROCODILE TEARS AND SALAMANDER SLIME

News of Grandfather's big trip traveled fast. Soon, all of my coworkers were back behind their desks. They were **happy** to be working at *The Rodent's Gazette* once more. I was happy, too. I'd forgotten how much I missed their furry faces! Finally, everything was back to normal.

One afternoon, the phone rang. "Hellooo! Long-distance call from Egypt for Mr. Stilton!" the operator squeaked.

"Yes, this is Stilton speaking, *Geronimo Stilton*," I said.

There was a crackling on the line.

Then a distant voice squeaked, "Geronimo! It's **ALRAT SPITFUR**."

My heart did a tap dance. The professor remembered me! Maybe he had remembered about his experiment, too!

"Professor! It's so great to hear from you!" I replied. Ever since I had returned from Egypt, I couldn't stop thinking about it. It really was a fascinating country.

The professor thanked me again for saving his life. He told me that he remembered everything. Except for one small detail.

He couldn't remember the **MYSTERIOUS** ingredient he had added to the camel dung.

"As soon as I identify it, though, I'll let you know," the professor assured me. "You can have the first interview."

I grinned. Somehow I knew I'd be hearing from him again.

"I wonder whether the secret ingredient was scorpion pee or salamander slime?" Professor Spitfur rambled on. "Or maybe it was crocodile tears? Anyway, I'm doing

some **experiments** now. In fact, I'm about to read a story to a crocodile. It has to be so sad it will bring tears to his eyes. What do you think, Stilton? Should I try **THE LITTLE MATCH RAT** or

Snow White and the Seven Mouslets?"

I smiled under my whiskers. What a character, that Alrat Spitfur.

WE'LL MAKE
MEGABUCKS!

I put down the receiver. Then I opened my desk drawer. I glanced at the pictures I had taken in the desert.

Ah, Egypt. It really was an unbelievable country.

And my pictures weren't bad, either! A pink dawn, the sand dunes, CHEOPS's pyramid . . .

Just then, Shif T. Paws strolled into my office. "Mr. Stilton, why don't you write an **ADVENTURE STORY** set in *Egypt*?" he squeaked.

I took another peek at the pictures. "You think I should, Shif?" I said.

The salesmouse jumped to his paws. "I do, I do!" he cried. "When it's published, we'll make **megabucks!** Trust me!"

I had to laugh. I could almost see the dollar signs shining in Shif T.'s beady little eyes.

I decided to write the book just for fun. And let me tell you, that salesmouse has some nose for business. The book was a **HUGE SUCCESS!** I called it *The Curse of the Cheese Pyramid.* It's the book you're reading right now! Yes, you are holding a genuine *Geronimo Stilton* bestseller!

GRANDFATHER AGAIN???

Days, weeks, months went by.

Very early one morning, I was fast asleep under my comfy, cozy blankets, snoring away.

Suddenly, the phone rang.

Ring! Ring! Ring! Ring! Ring! Ring!

I got out of bed half asleep, sinking my paws into my cat-fur rug. *Still soft as ever,* I thought.

I reached for the phone. "Hello! Stilton speaking, *Geronimo Stilton,*" I mumbled.

A strangely familiar-sounding voice shrieked back at me. "WAKE UP! WAAAKE UUUUUP!"

My ears started ringing like the ice cream

rat's truck in the summertime. "W-who . . . w-what . . . who is it?" I stammered.

I glanced at the alarm clock. GREASY CAT GUTS! It was two o'clock in the morning!

Grandfather William's squeak blasted my eardrum.

"Grandson! I'm calling from Timbuktu!" he screamed. "I've just heard that Professor SPITFUR has remembered the secret ingredient. He'll be calling you any minute now. You must interview him immediately! I've booked you a flight to Egypt!"

My eyes opened wide. Oh, no, not Dirt Cheap Airlines again! I wasn't sure my nerves could stand another flight like that. But Grandfather wasn't talking about a plane this time. It was worse. Much worse. "To save money, you'll be taking a hot-air balloon!" he squeaked.

"Now, get packed and get moving! Remember, time is money and money is time!"

Then he slammed the receiver down in my ear.

I groaned. **Rat-munching rattlesnakes**! I was ready to get back under the blankets and go on snoring. But then I saw my pictures of Egypt on my bedside table. I remembered the desert and the sunsets and the pyramids and the camels. OK, so maybe I wasn't so crazy about those camels, but I did have one **AMAZING ADVENTURE**.

I pulled out my suitcase and began to pack. Yes, I, *Geronimo Stilton*, was headed back to Egypt.

But that's another story. . . .

ABOUT THE AUTHOR

Born in New Mouse City, Mouse Island, Geronimo Stilton is Rattus Emeritus of Mousomorphic Literature and of Neo-Ratonic Comparative Philosophy. For the past twenty years, he has been running *The Rodent's Gazette*, New Mouse City's most widely read daily newspaper.

Stilton was awarded the Ratitzer Prize for his scoop on *The Curse of the Cheese Pyramid*. He has also received the Andersen 2000 Prize for Personality of the Year. One of his bestsellers won the 2002 eBook Award for world's best ratlings' electronic book. His works have been published in 180 countries.

In his spare time, Mr. Stilton collects antique cheese rinds and plays golf. But what he most enjoys is telling stories to his nephew Benjamin.

Don't miss any of my other fabumouse adventures!

#1
Lost Treasure of
the Emerald Eye

#3
Cat and Mouse in a
Haunted House

#4
I'm Too Fond
of My Fur!

and coming soon

#5
Four Mice Deep in
the Jungle

Want to read my next adventure?
It's sure to be a fur-raising experience!

CAT AND MOUSE IN A HAUNTED HOUSE

Lost in a dark, spooky forest! It was truly a fur-raising experience for a 'fraidy-mouse like me. So I sought shelter for the night in a crumbling old castle. The place was completely empty . . . or so I thought. But I quickly discovered that it was haunted—by cats! Holey cheese, cats give me mouse bumps! Let me tell you, this was one case where curiosity almost killed the mouse. . . .

THE RODENT'S GAZETTE

1. **Main Entrance**

2. **Printing presses (where the books and newspaper are printed)**

3. **Accounts department**

4. **Editorial room (where the editors, illustrators, and designers work)**

5. **Geronimo Stilton's office**

6. **Storage space for Geronimo's books**

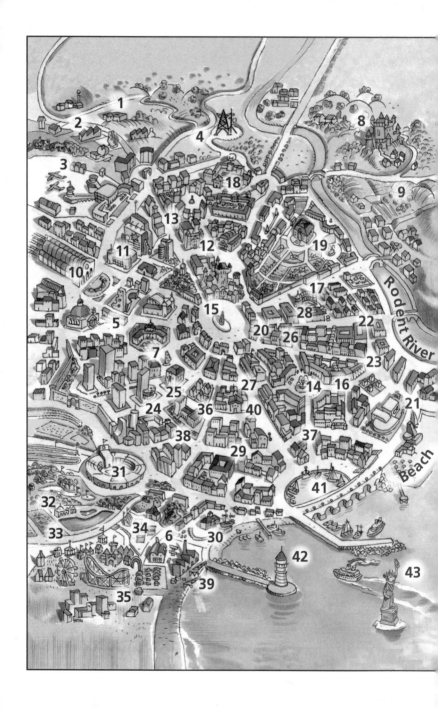

Map of New Mouse City

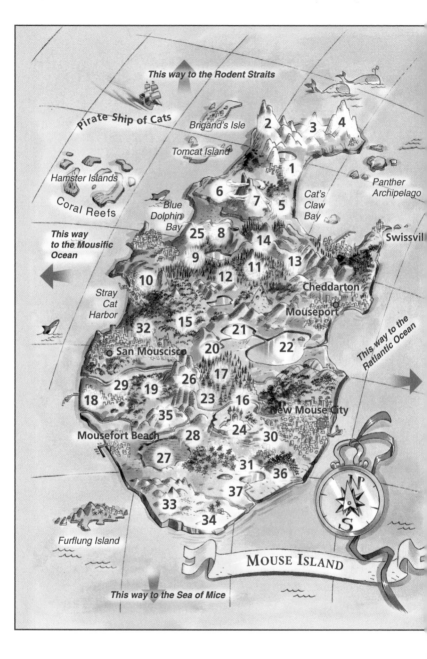

Map of Mouse Island

1. Big Ice Lake
2. Frozen Fur Peak
3. Slipperyslopes Glacier
4. Coldcreeps Peak
5. Ratzikistan
6. Transratania
7. Mount Vamp
8. Roastedrat Volcano
9. Brimstone Lake
10. Poopedcat Pass
11. Stinko Peak
12. Dark Forest
13. Vain Vampires Valley
14. Goose Bumps Gorge
15. The Shadow Line Pass
16. Penny Pincher Lodge
17. Nature Reserve Park
18. Las Ratayas Marinas
19. Fossil Forest
20. Lake Lake
21. Lake Lake Lake
22. Lake Lakelakelake
23. Cheddar Crag
24. Cannycat Castle
25. Valley of the Giant Sequoia
26. Cheddar Springs
27. Sulfurous Swamp
28. Old Reliable Geyser
29. Vole Vail
30. Ravingrat Ravine
31. Gnat Marshes
32. Munster Highlands
33. Mousehara Desert
34. Oasis of the Sweaty Camel
35. Cabbagehead Hill
36. Tropical Jungle
37. Rio Mosquito

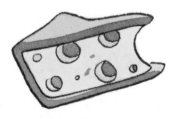

Dear mouse friends,
thanks for reading, and farewell
till the next book.
It'll be another whisker-licking-good
adventure, and that's a promise!

Geronimo Stilton